easych

ssential guitar chords

jeromy bessler and norbert opgenoorth

$3\,{}^{50}_{G9}$

Voggenreiter

Voggenreiter Publishers
Viktoriastr. 25, 53173 Bonn/Germany
www.voggenreiter.de
info@voggenreiter.de

ISBN: 3-8024-0362-2

Contents

I. Preface

This booklet contains the most important guitar chords in an easy-to-use graphical format. We have tried to pick the most common chords and practical voicings from the vast number of guitar chords that are theoretically possible.

These chords are arranged chromatically ascending from C. In each key, the chords are arranged according to their chord-type.

Chords that can be spelled enharmonically (G♯ and A♭, for example) are only notated with flats; F♯ being the only exception.
All fingerings given are just suggestions and may be changed to suit your own taste or playing style.

Chord diagrams

In the chord diagrams used here (and in most other books), horizontal lines are representing the strings of the guitar (counting from the low E-string up to the high E-string). Vertical lines are representing the frets.
The fingers of the left hand (or the right if you're left-handed) are numbered:

1 = index finger
2 = middle finger
3 = ring finger
4 = little finger

Open strings are indicated by an "o" to the left of the chord diagram; muted or not picked strings (meaning all strings that shouldn't sound) are indicated by an "x". The position (the fret on the fretboard) of a chord is given below the chord diagram.

This chord diagram for a Cmaj7-chord reads as follows:

The low E-string is muted / not picked. The middle finger frets the A-string at the third fret, the index finger frets the D-string at the second fret.
G-, B-, and high E-string are played as open strings.

Bar-chords (chords using one finger to fret two or more strings at the same time) are indicated with a beam across all the strings used for the bar.
Again, the finger used for the bar is indicated:

II. The most impor-tant chords

Basic chords

These are the most basic guitar chords.
All fingerings are just suggestions and may be changed if necessary.

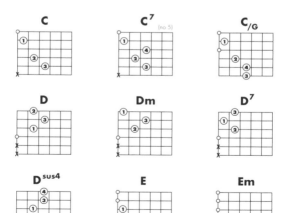

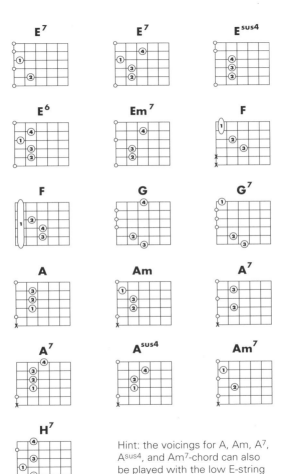

Hint: the voicings for A, Am, A^7, A^{sus4}, and Am^7-chord can also be played with the low E-string not muted.

Root
C

C

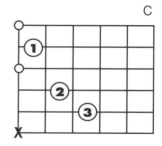

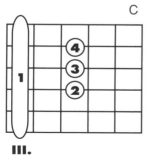

III.

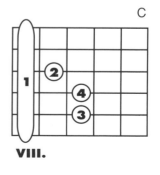

VIII.

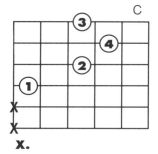

C

Cm

x.

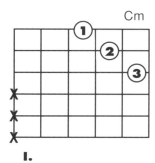

Cm

I.

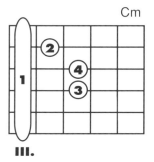

Cm

III.

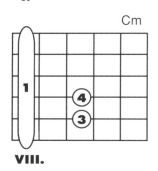

Cm

VIII.

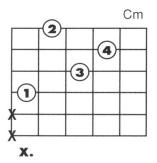

Cm

x.

9

C⁷

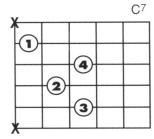

C⁷

I.

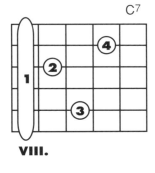

C⁷

VIII.

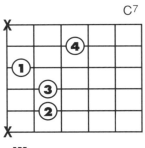

C⁷

IX.

Cmaj7

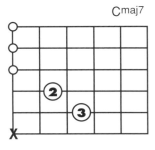

Cmaj7

I.

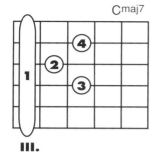

C^{maj7}

III.

Cm⁷

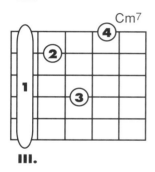

Cm⁷

III.

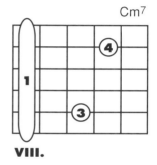

Cm⁷

VIII.

C⁶

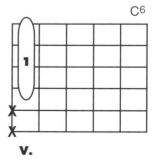

C⁶

V.

11

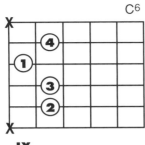

C⁶

Cm⁶

IX.

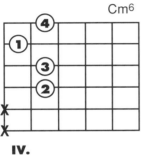

Cm⁶

Cˢᵘˢ⁴

IV.

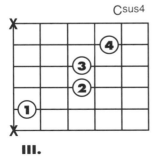

Cˢᵘˢ⁴

III.

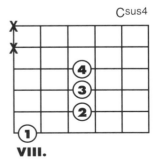

Cˢᵘˢ⁴

VIII.

12

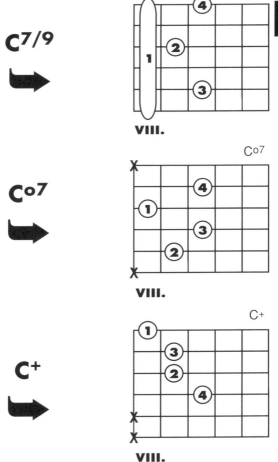

C⁷ᐟ⁹

C7/9

VIII.

Cᵒ⁷

Co7

VIII.

C⁺

C+

VIII.

13

Root
C♯/D♭

D♭

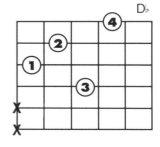

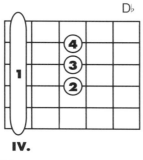

IV.

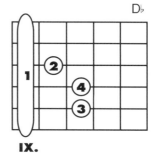

IX.

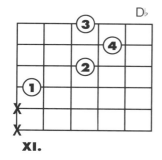

XI.

D♭m

C♯/D♭

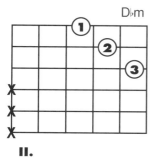

II.

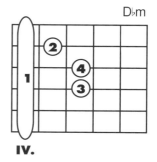

IV.

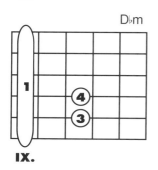

IX.

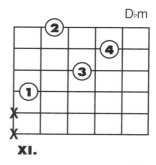

XI.

C#/Db

Db7

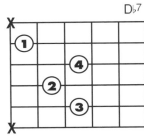

II.

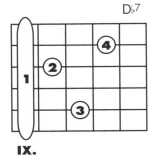

IX.

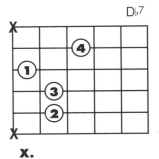

X.

Dbmaj7

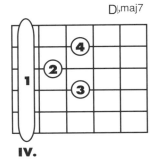

IV.

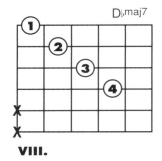

D♭maj7

VIII.

D♭m⁷

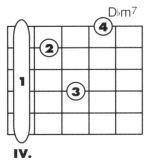

D♭m⁷

IV.

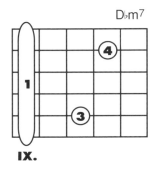

D♭m⁷

IX.

D♭6

D♭6

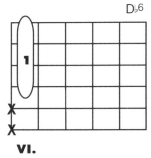

D♭6

VI.

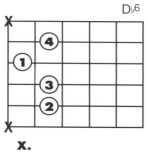

D♭6

X.

D♭m6

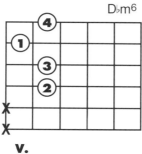

D♭m6

V.

D♭sus4

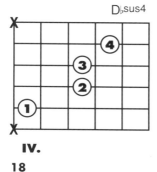

D♭sus4

IV.

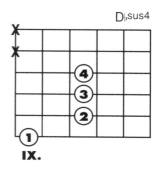

D♭sus4

IX.

C♯/D♭

18

D♭7/9

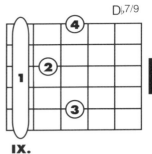

D♭7/9

IX.

D♭o7

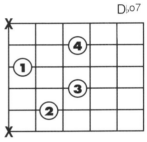

D♭o7

IX.

D♭+

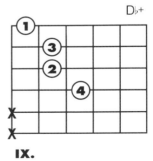

D♭+

IX.

19

Root
D

D

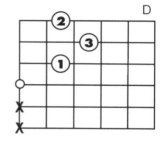

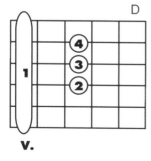

v.

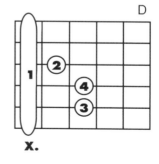

x.

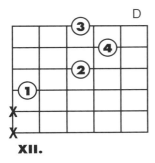

Dm

XII.

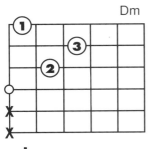

I.

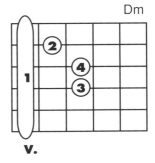

V.

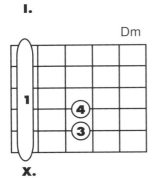

X.

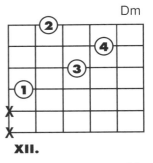

XII.

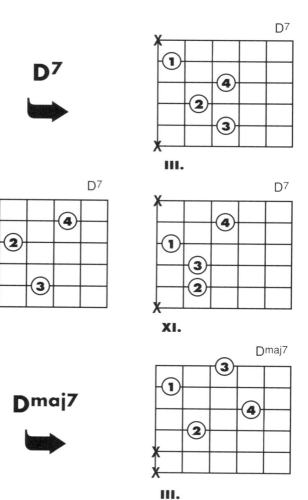

D⁷

D⁷

III.

D⁷

X.

D⁷

XI.

Dmaj7

Dmaj7

III.

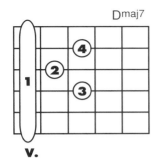

Dmaj7

Dm7

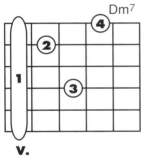

Dm7

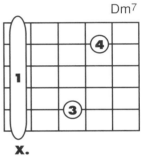

Dm7

D6

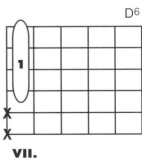

D6

D

23

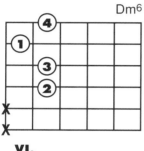

D6

XI.

Dm6

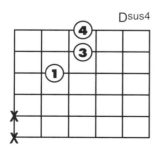

Dm6

VI.

Dsus4

Dsus4

Dsus4

V.

D⁷/⁹

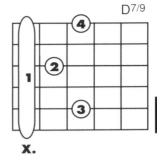

D

D°⁷

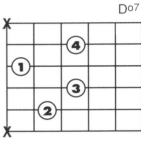

D⁺

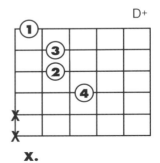

Root
D♯/E♭

E♭

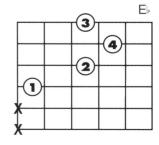

E♭

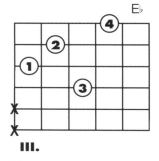

III.

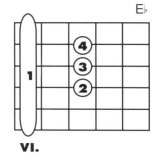

VI.

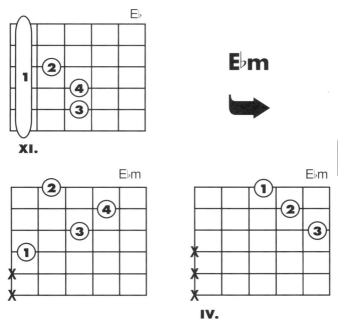

E♭m

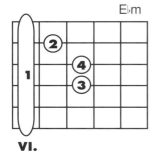

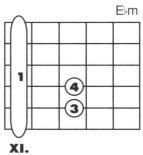

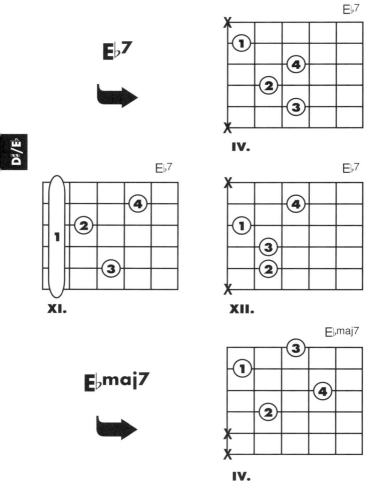

E♭7

E♭maj7

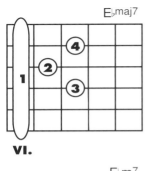

E♭maj7

VI.

E♭m7

D#/E♭

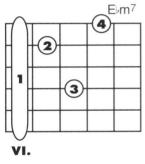

E♭m7

VI.

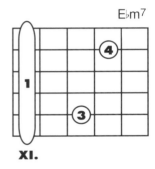

E♭m7

XI.

E♭6

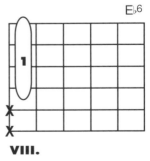

E♭6

VIII.

E♭6

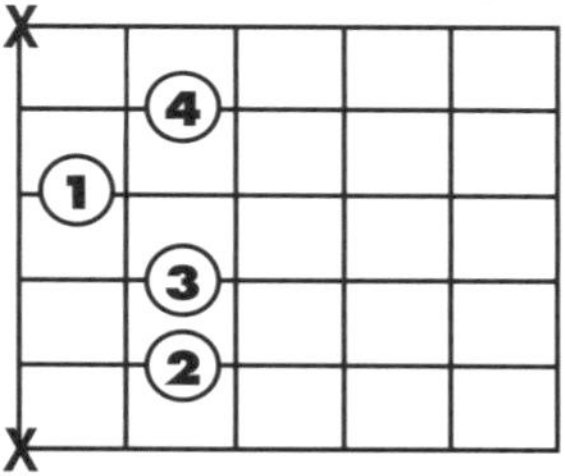

XII.

E♭m⁶

➥

E♭m6

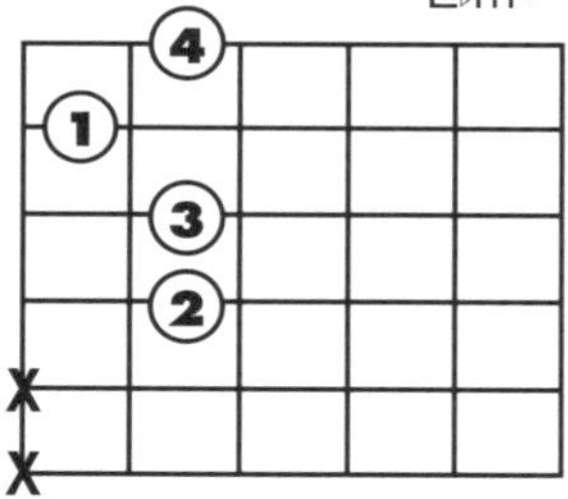

VII.

E♭sus4

➥

E♭sus4

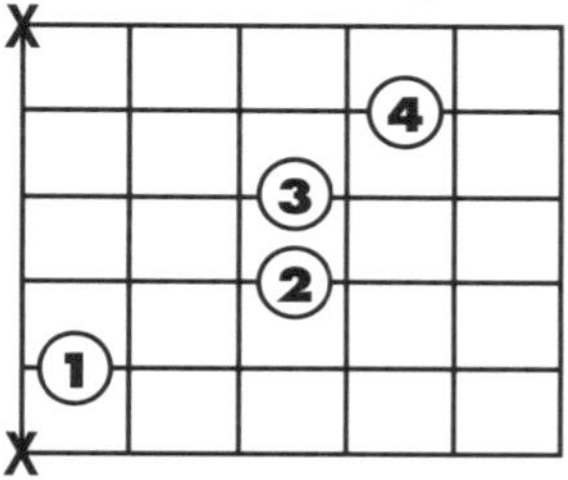

VI.

E♭sus4

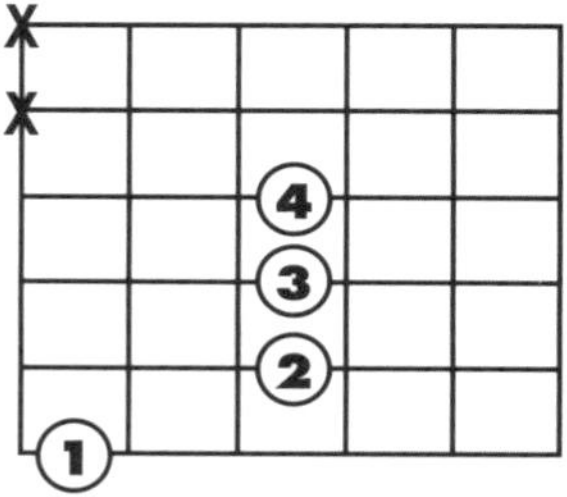

XI.

E♭7/9

➥

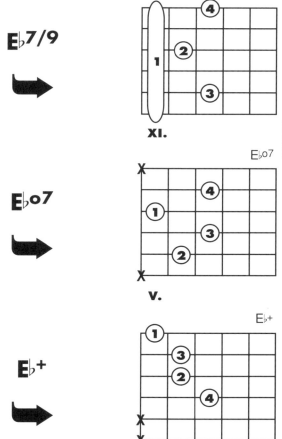

E♭7/9

XI.

E♭o7

➥

E♭o7

V.

E♭+

➥

E♭+

XI.

D♯/E♭

31

Root
E

E

E ↩

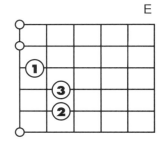

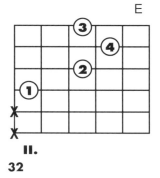

II.

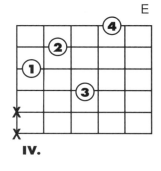

IV.

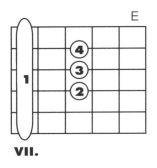

Em

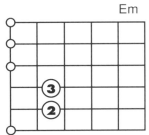

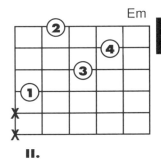

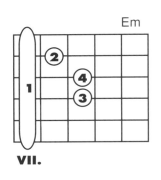

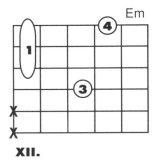

33

E⁷ ➡

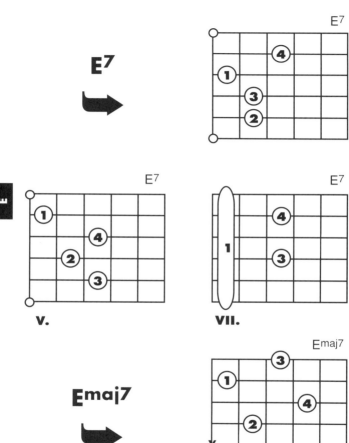

E⁷

E⁷   V.

E⁷   VII.

Emaj7 ➡

Emaj7   V.

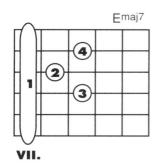

E^maj7

VII.

Em^7

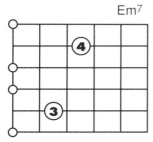

Em^7

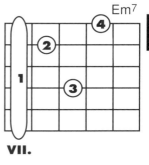

Em^7

VII.

E^6

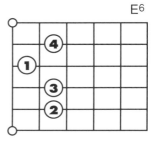

E^6

35

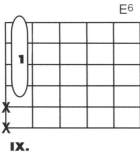

E⁶

Em⁶

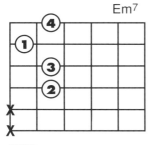

Em⁷

Esus4

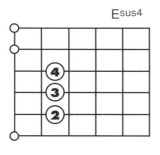

Esus4

Esus4

E

36

E⁷/⁹

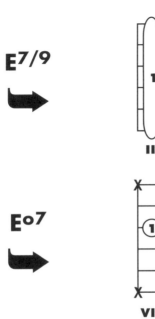

$E^{7/9}$

II.

E°7

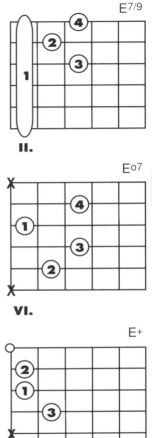

E^{o7}

VI.

E

E⁺

E^{+}

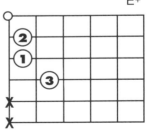

Root
F

F

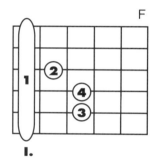

I.

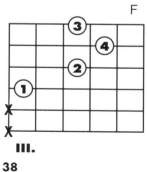

III.

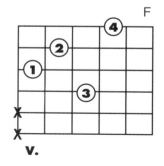

V.

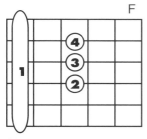

F

VIII.

Fm

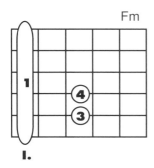

Fm

I.

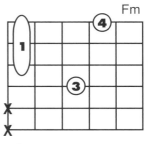

Fm

I.

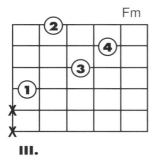

Fm

III.

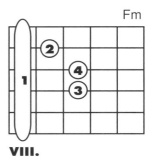

Fm

VIII.

F7

F7

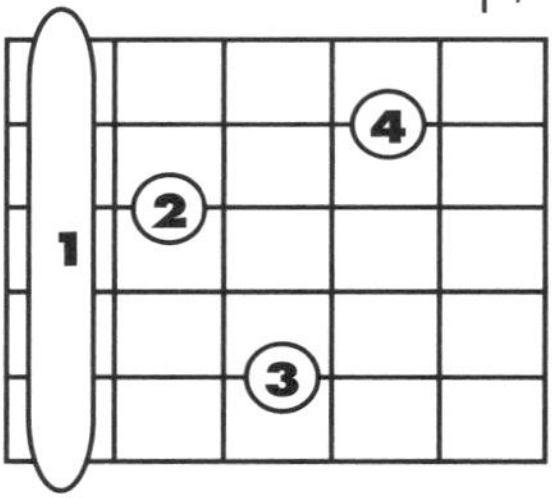

I.

F7

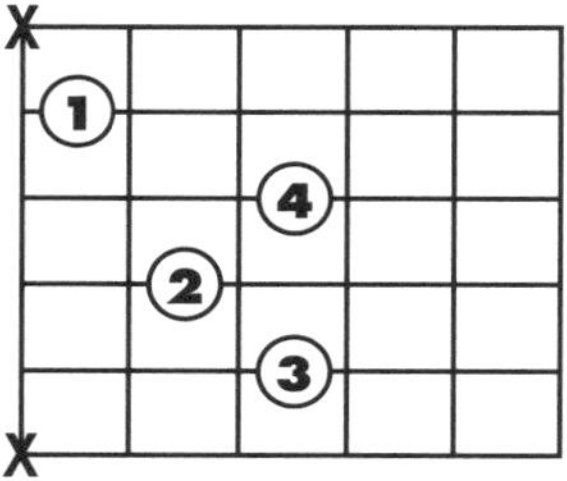

VI.

F7

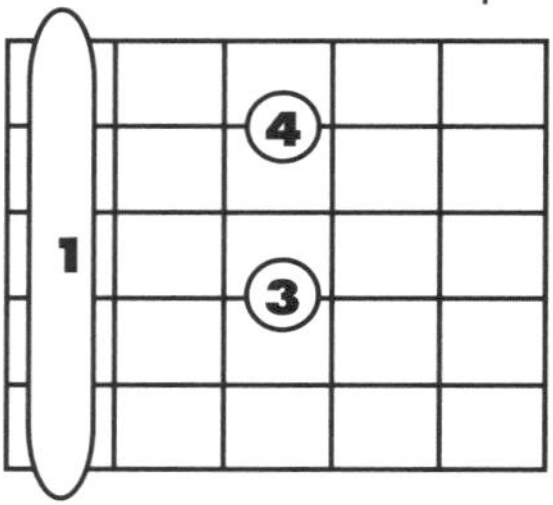

VIII.

Fmaj7

Fmaj7

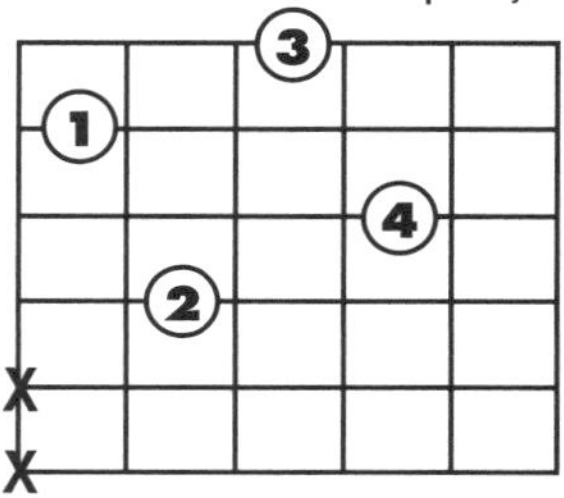

VI.

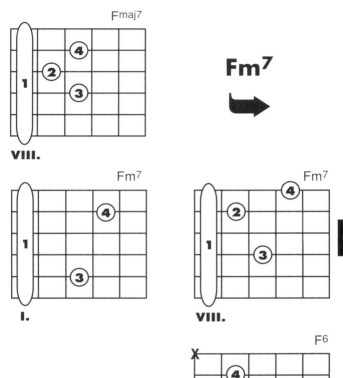

Fmaj7

Fm⁷

Fm⁷
I.

Fm⁷
VIII.

F⁶

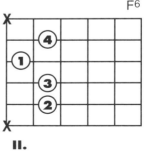

F⁶
II.

F6

Fm⁶

X.

Fm⁶

Fsus4

IX.

Fsus4

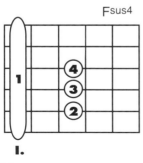

I.

Fsus4

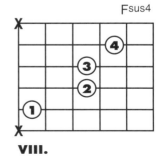

VIII.

42

F⁷ᐟ⁹

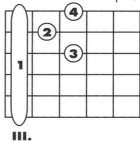

F7/9

III.

Fº7

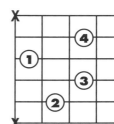

Fo7

VII.

F⁺

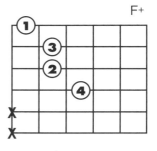

F+

F

43

Root
F#/G♭

F#

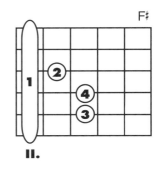

II.

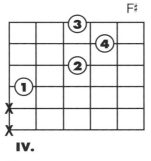

IV.

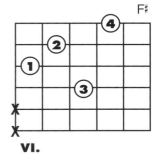

VI.

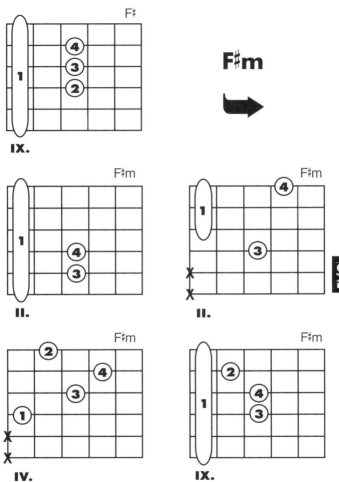

F#m

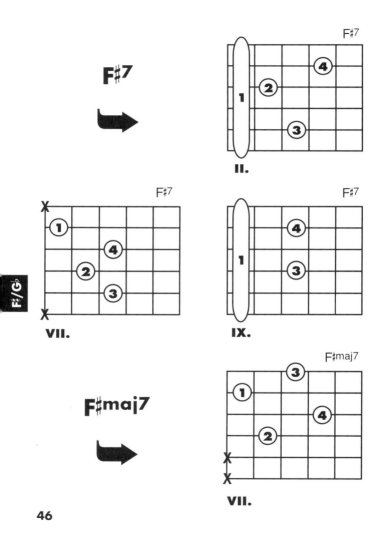

F#7

F#7

II.

F#7

VII.

F#7

IX.

F#maj7

F#maj7

VII.

F#maj7

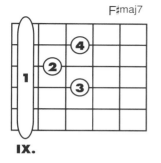

IX.

F#m7

F#m7

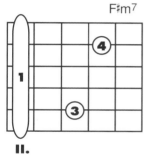

II.

F#m7

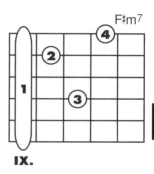

IX.

F#/G♭

F#6

F#6

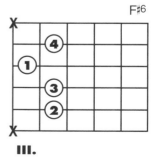

III.

47

F#6

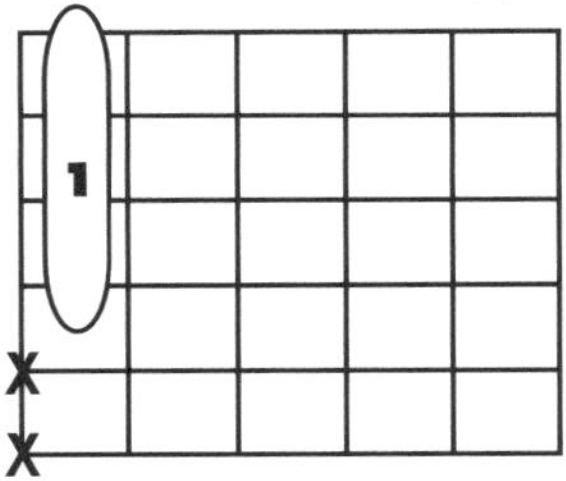

XI.

F#m 6

F#m6

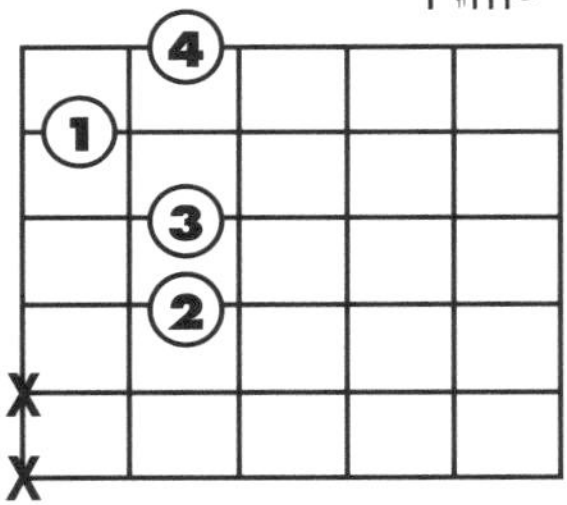

X.

F#sus4

F#sus4

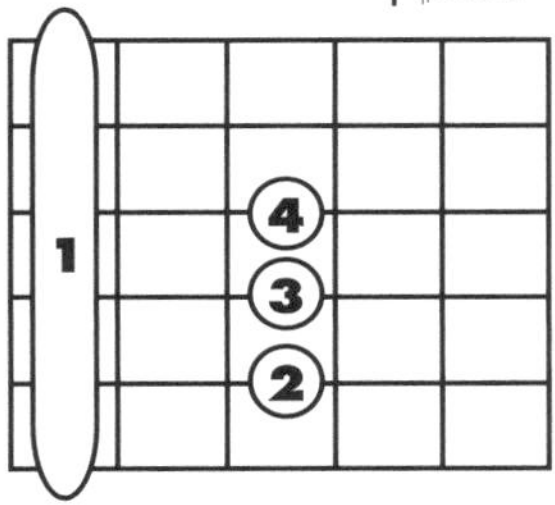

II.

F#sus4

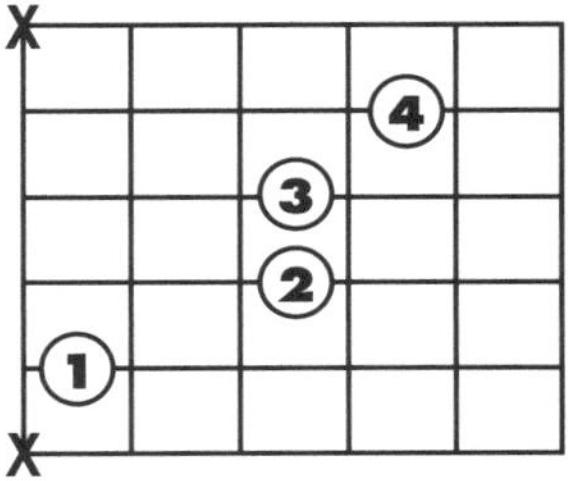

IX.

F#/G♭

F#7/9

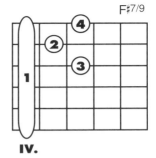

F#7/9

IV.

F#o7

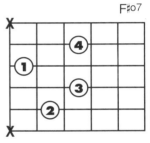

F#o7

VIII.

F#/Gb

F#+

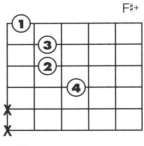

F#+

II.

49

Root G

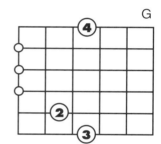

G

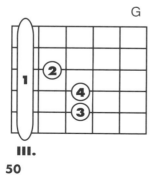

III.

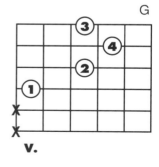

V.

50

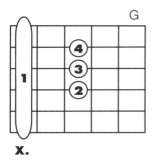

x.

Gm

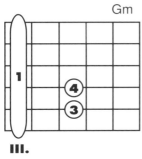

III.

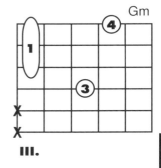

III.

G

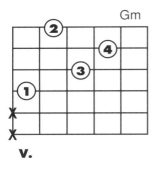

v.

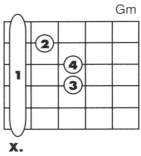

x.

51

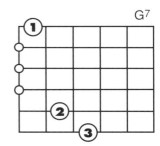

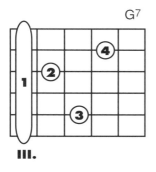

III.

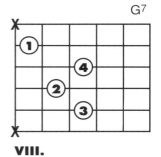

VIII.

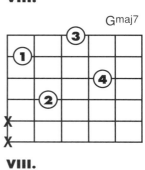

VIII.

G

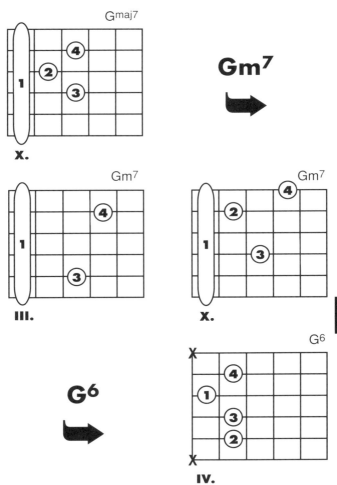

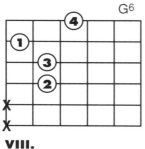

G6

VIII.

Gm6

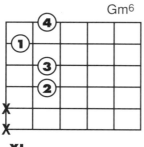

Gm6

XI.

Gsus4

G

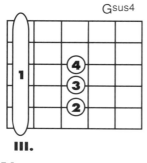

Gsus4

III.

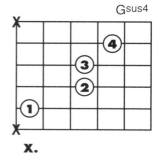

Gsus4

X.

54

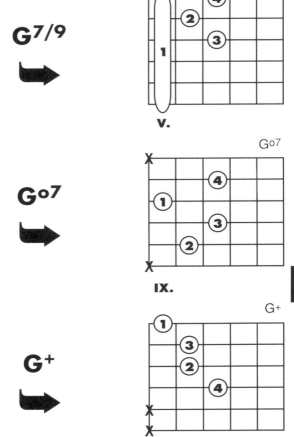

G⁷/⁹

$G^{7/9}$

V.

G°7

G^{o7}

IX.

G⁺

G^+

III.

G

Root
G♯/A♭

A♭

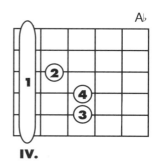

IV.

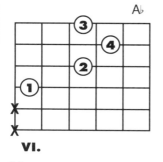

VI.

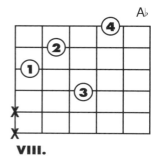

VIII.

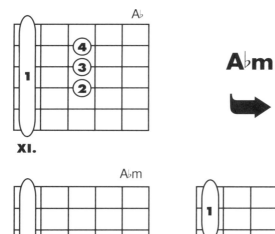

A♭m

➡

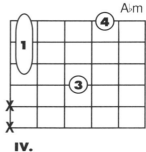

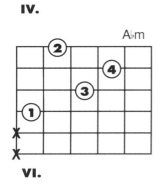

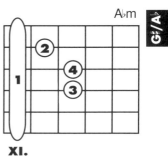

G♯/A♭

57

A♭7

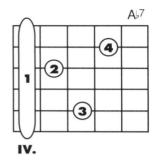

A♭7

IV.

A♭7

IX.

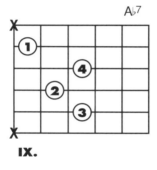

A♭7

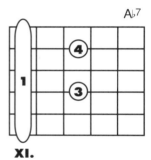

XI.

A♭maj7

A♭maj7

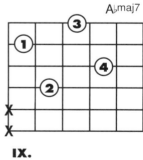

IX.

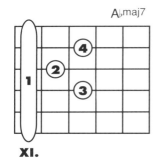

A♭maj7

XI.

A♭m⁷

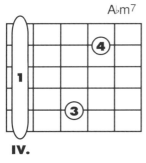

A♭m⁷

IV.

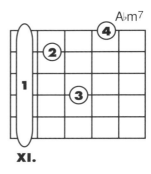

A♭m⁷

XI.

A♭6

G#/A♭

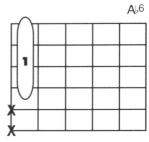

A♭6

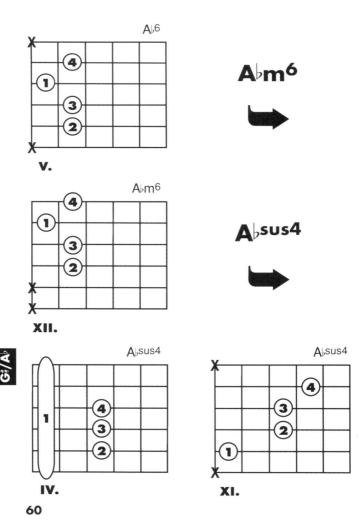

A♭6

A♭m6

V.

A♭m6

A♭sus4

XII.

A♭sus4

IV.

A♭sus4

XI.

G♯/A♭

60

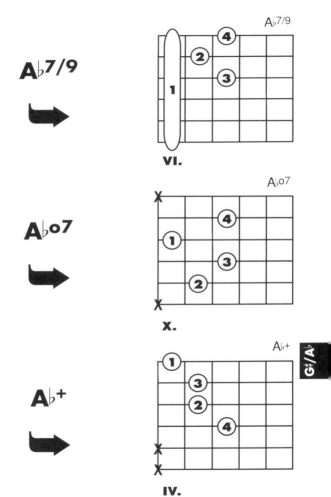

A♭7/9

A♭o7

A♭+

61

Root
A

A

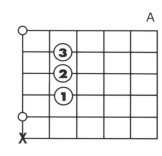

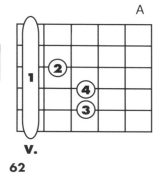

V.

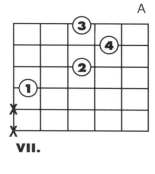

VII.

62

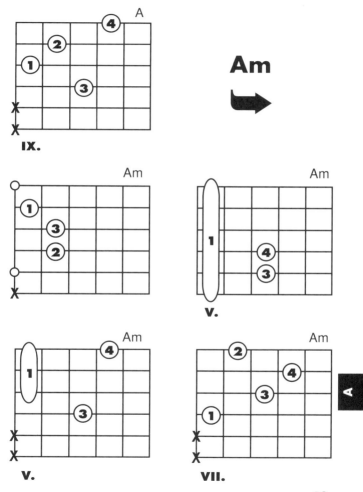

Am

63

A⁷

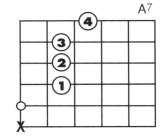

A⁷

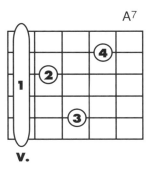

A⁷   v.

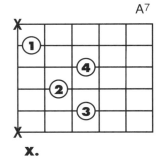

A⁷   x.

 Amaj7

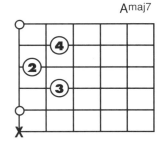

Amaj7

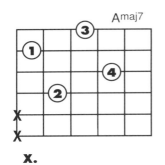

A^maj7

X.

Am^7

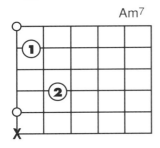

Am^7

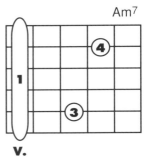

Am^7

V.

A^6

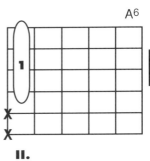

A^6

II.

A

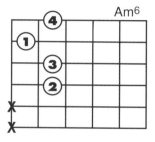

A⁶

VI.

Am⁶

Am⁶

Aˢᵘˢ⁴

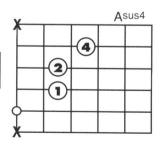

Aˢᵘˢ⁴

A

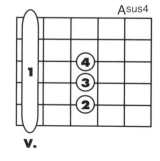

Aˢᵘˢ⁴

V.

A⁷/⁹

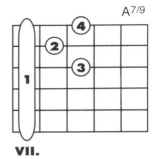

A⁷/⁹

VII.

A°7

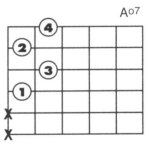

A°7

VII.

A⁺

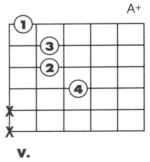

A⁺

V.

Root
A♯/B

B♭

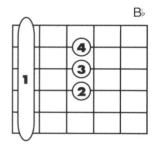

B♭

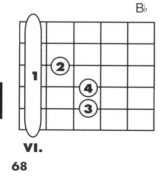

VI.

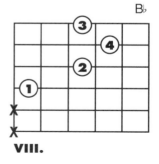

VIII.

A♯/B♭

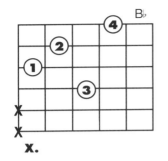

X.

B♭m

B♭m

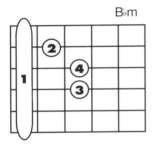

VI.

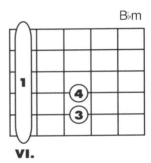

VI.

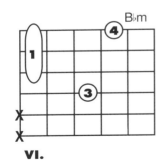

VI.

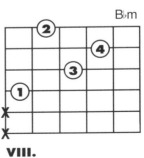

VIII.

A♯/B♭

69

B♭7

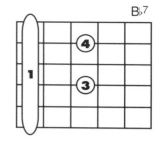

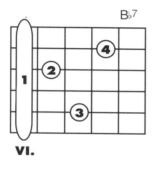

VI.

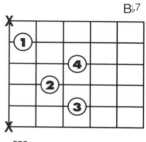

XI.

 B♭maj7

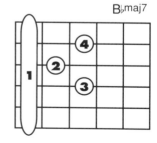

 A♯/B♭

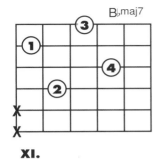

B♭maj7

XI.

B♭m⁷

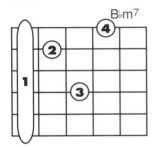

B♭m⁷

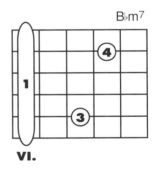

B♭m⁷

VI.

B♭6

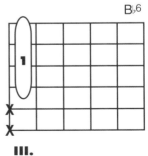

B♭6

III.

A♯/B♭

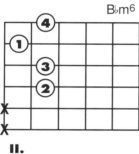

B♭6

VII.

B♭m⁶

B♭m⁶

II.

B♭sus4

B♭sus4

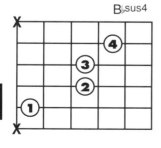

B♭sus4

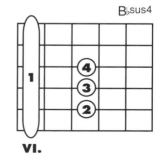

VI.

A#/B♭

B♭7/9

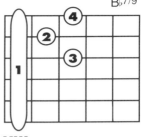

B♭7/9

VIII.

B♭o7

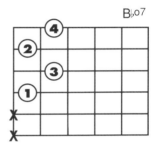

B♭o7

VIII.

B♭+

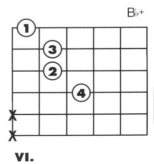

B♭+

VI.

A♯/B♭

73

Root
B

B

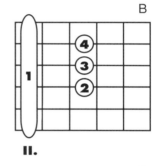

II.

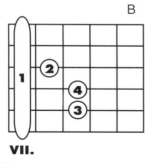

VII.

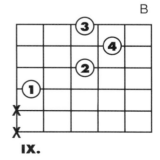

IX.

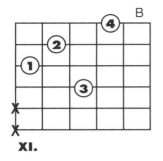

Bm

XI.

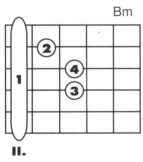

II.

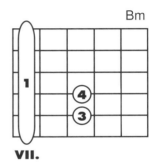

VII.

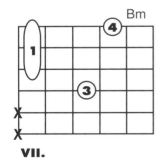

VII.

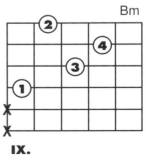

IX.

B

B⁷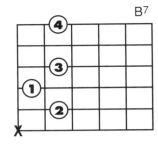

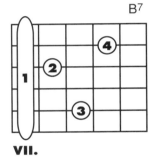

Bmaj7

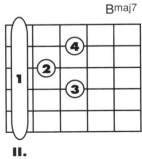

B

76

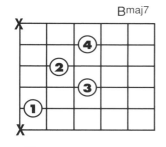

B^{maj7}

II.

Bm⁷

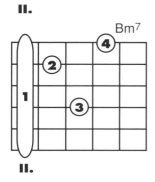

Bm⁷

II.

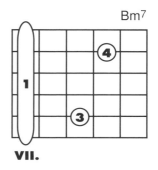

Bm⁷

VII.

B⁶

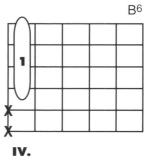

B⁶

IV.

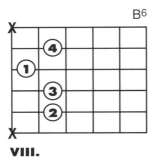

B⁶ → B^6

VIII.

Bm^6 →

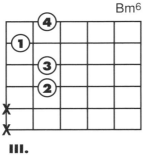

Bm^6

III.

B^{sus4} →

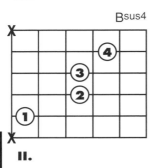

B^{sus4}

II.

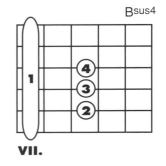

B^{sus4}

VII.

B

78

B⁷/⁹

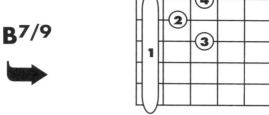

B7/9

IX.

B°7

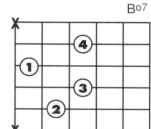

B°7

B⁺

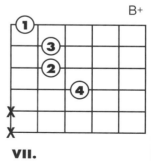

B⁺

VII.

B

III. Chord symbols

Symbol	Chord structure
major	1 - 3 - 5
6	1 - 3 - 5 - 6
sus4	1 - 4 - 5
maj7	1 - 3 - 5 - 7
m	1 - ♭3 - 5
m 6	1 - ♭3 - 5 - 6
m 7	1 - ♭3 - 5 - ♭7
7	1 - 3 - 5 - ♭7
7 / 9	1 - 3 - 5 - ♭7 - 9
o7	1 - ♭3 - ♭5 - ♭♭7
+	1 - 3 - ♯5